WILLIAM WEGMAN'S

# FARM DAYS

*or*

HOW CHIP LEARNT AN
IMPORTANT LESSON ON THE FARM

*OR*

## A DAY IN THE COUNTRY

*OR*

HIP CHIP'S TRIP

OR

FARMER BOY

HYPERION • NEW YORK

# City Boy Chip had been

invited by his country cousins, the McDoubles, to visit

them on the farm. They were supposed to meet him at

the station.

## "Where are they? They must be very busy

with farm chores," thought Chip.

# Batty and Crooky McDouble lived on

the old McFay farm, owned and operated by Farmer Chundo McFay.

It was a big farm with many barns and fields and pastures where cows

and horses could graze and wander about.

Chip set off to find the farm. The McDoubles
had said it was just a mile from the station.

# Which way?

## This way?

# No . . . maybe this way.

He wasn't sure. "There's a cow," he thought.
"I must be getting close."

## "Hello. Is this the McFay farm?"

asked Chip.

"This is the McFay farm all right. Yup it is, E-I-E-I-O,

and I am Farmer Chundo McFay.

## Jiggity jig, help me down. What's your name?"

"Chip," he replied.

"Chip! What kind of a wacky name is that? Bless my ketchup bottle.

You must be the city boy the McDoubles were telling me about.

Hot diggity. Gitty git giggity."

Chip liked Farmer Chundo. He was tall and friendly and

a little hard to understand.

Farmer Chundo seated himself on a big red tractor and started it with a crank. It made a lot of noise. "So the McDoubles tell me you want to be a farmer. Do you like vegetables? Do you like broccoli, green beans, peppers, squash, and that sort of thing? Well then, hop on! The McDoubles are out in the big field planting a garden."

# Lickity plickity and off they rode,

over the hill and down to the big field to find the McDoubles.

**"Hi, Chip,"** said Batty.

**"Hi, Chip,"** said Crooky.

"Sorry we couldn't meet you at the station. We had to pick up seeds and supplies. We're going to make a vegetable garden. It will be fun, and we could sure use some help."

"There's a wheelbarrow over there," said Batty.

"And here's a shovel," said Crooky.

"OK," said Chip good-naturedly.

"Let's see, peas and carrots along this row here and broccoli there. Cucumbers over here and tomatoes back there. Or maybe the other way around," said Crooky.

## "What about squash?" said Batty.

## "Squash is OK, but I prefer watermelons," said Crooky.

Chip dug the garden, carted away all the heavy rocks with the wheelbarrow, and set up the fence. The McDoubles planted the seeds.

"Hippity hoe, nice work, youngsters," said Farmer Chundo.
"Now make sure you give your garden plenty of water."

# Chundo told the youngsters that planting was just the beginning.

"To grow healthy vegetables, keep in mind the four Ws: Watering, weeding, and waiting."

"That's only three," said Chip.

"Whatever," said Farmer Chundo.

"Oh," said Chip. "Watering, weeding, waiting, and whatever."

Farmer Chundo showed them what they could expect to see in their garden if they cared for it properly. The little seeds would grow into big watermelons, giant cauliflower, jumbo tomatoes, long green beans, and huge peas.

Chip wondered when he could begin weeding.

"I hear cows a-calling," said Farmer Chundo. "How'd you like to milk a cow, Chip?"

"I like milk," said Chip.

## THE FOUR Ws:

Watering

Weeding

Waiting

and

Whatever...

Farmer Chundo drove everyone over to the cow barn on his
tractor. When they got there, the McDoubles sat right down
to enjoy a carton of fresh milk from their prize cow.

"Mmmmmm...Milk," said Batty.

"Mmmmmm...Milk," said Crooky.

"Which cow should I milk?" asked Chip.

"There's more to milking cows than milking cows," said Farmer
Chundo. Chip and Farmer Chundo went into the barn to clean the
stalls. Chip was a little afraid. The cows were really big.

After a big lunch at the farmhouse, Farmer Chundo
led the trio back out to the big field.

"The hay needs mowing," said Farmer Chundo.

Batty and Crooky showed Chip how to use the mower.

# "You just push," said Batty.
# "And just keep pushing," said Crooky.

# "...and pushing."

Meanwhile, the McDoubles went down to the pond to check on the ducks. They decided to check on the fish, too.

Chip continued to mow and mow and mow and mow, mow, mow, mow, mow.

Later that afternoon, Farmer Chundo was pitching hay when he heard a strange sound.

# "Bumblebees? Sawing? What's that noise?"

Exhausted from mowing, Chip had fallen asleep in a nice soft pile of hay. He was very comfortable.

"Wake up, youngster. Chippity cricket. No time for naps on a farm. Crows in the corn, cows in the barn . . . or something. There are still more chores to do. Here, Chip, put on my hat."

## "I still don't see any crows," said Chip.

"He's doing a good job," said Batty.

"Chip looks really scary," said Crooky.